THE CHRISTMAS PLAY

OTHER LOYOLA PRESS TITLES
BY CAROL LYNN PEARSON

A Christmas Thief: A Novel

The Modern Magi: A Christmas Novel

A Stranger for Christmas: A Novel

LOYOLAPRESS.

3441 N. ASHLAND AVENUE
CHICAGO, ILLINOIS 60657
(800) 621-1008
WWW.LOYOLABOOKS.ORG

Illustration by Anni Betts
Jacket and interior design by Laura Steur

Library of Congress Cataloging-in-Publication Data
Pearson, Carol Lynn.
    The Christmas play : a fable for the holidays / Carol Lynn Pearson.
       p. cm.
    ISBN 0-8294-1942-X
    1. Christmas plays—Presentation, etc.—Fiction. I. Title.
PS3566.E227C48 2004
813'.54—dc22

                                                    2004001510

Printed in Mexico
04 05 06 07 08 09 10 11 RRD 10 9 8 7 6 5 4 3 2 1

CAROL LYNN PEARSON

THE CHRISTMAS PLAY

A Fable for the Holidays

Illustrated by Anni Betts

LOYOLAPRESS.

CHICAGO

The sign at the neighborhood theater read:

I went inside and up onto the stage, alone. The spotlight was bright, nearly blinding, and I raised a hand to shield my eyes.

A Voice came from the darkness, full and rich. "You wish to try out for my play?"

Feeling butterflies, I replied, "I do. I've always wanted to be in the Christmas story."

"Wonderful!" sounded the Voice brightly. "The play begins with the angel. I bet you'd be a fine angel. You do proclaim peace and good will, don't you? And bring good tidings of great joy? You don't complain a lot, do you?"

I looked down and dug the stage with my toe. "Well, I wouldn't call it a lot. . . ."

"How about angelic encounters? I'll bet people are always having experiences with you that leave them saying, 'That must have been an angel!'"

I chuckled, "'Angelic' is a bit much, don't you think? Would you settle for 'generally pleasant or congenial encounters'?"

The Voice was silent.

And then, still enthusiastic, the Voice said, "I also need a shepherd. Have you been keeping watch over your flock by night?"

"My flock?"

"You know, family, friends, strangers, that flock I gave you."

"Well, most days I . . ."

"No, no, no! By night!" The Voice, filled with tenderness, said, "When the hard things happen, to you, to them. Your flock is in safe hands, isn't it? The whole flock? Even the one?"

"Oh. Even the one . . . maybe not." I cringed and thought, "Especially if the one happened to be that telephone solicitor this morning."

After a pause, the Voice spoke again. "I need a wise man, too." Clearly this part was a favorite. I could hear the excitement building. "Tell me about following the star, about keeping your eye on the light and looking up, not down. Tell me about traveling reverently through the heart of every person I place in your path!"

"Through the heart of every one?" I asked. "Surely, you don't mean EVERY *one?"*

Silence.

I spoke again. "Is there another part?"

"There is, the one who gives birth." The Voice asked gently, "How are you at nurturing every good thought conceived in your mind? At birthing every good intention?"

Relieved, I said, "Oh, you mean doing things. Now that I'm good at. I've got my resume here."

"I'd rather hear you read the line on page twelve. Halfway down. The line about trust. I love this line. 'Be it unto me . . .' Go ahead."

Thumbing through the script, I found the page and cleared my throat. "Be it unto me according to thy word. . . . That one?"

"That one!" exclaimed the Voice. "But say it with a little more conviction. I like conviction."

"Be it unto me . . ." My voice cracked, and I peered out into the darkness. "Are there any other parts?"

"I need a good Joseph. Can you stand back and be supportive, going quietly about your work and not upstaging people? You don't need top billing, do you? Your name in lights? You're not here for the applause, are you?"

"Oh no, of course not. But, um, I'd still get my name in the program, wouldn't I?" I asked. "Somewhere?"

"And if you didn't?" the Voice asked kindly.

"Well, I . . . I was hoping for a little, you know, recognition?"

"There is another role I need to fill."
The Voice paused thoughtfully. "A very
demanding role—the Holy Child."

"Oh, I don't think . . ."

Full of hope, the Voice interrupted, "Can you
stand where he stood? Can you love, feel
compassion for, and forgive those who hate
you? Could you die for them?"

"Look. I don't know about . . ."

"May I hear the line at the top of page
forty-seven? It's one of my favorites."

I found the page, found the line. "Oh, wow. This one is almost impossible."

"Yes, almost."

I muttered under my breath, "And I suppose I should say it with conviction. . . ."

I took a deep breath. "Love your enemies. . . ."

"Ah! Such a great line!"

"Do good to them which hate you. . . ."

"Can you give me a little more passion?"

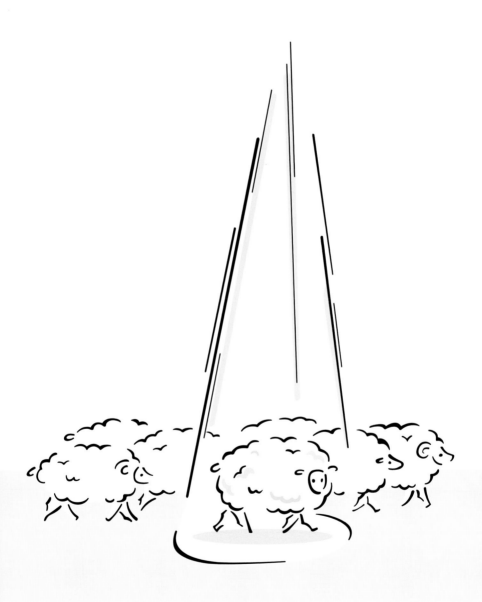

I sighed and peered into the darkness, "Do you need a sheep?"

The Voice thundered, "No one needs a sheep! I need a star!"

I backed away from the light, "Ok, clearly this was a mistake. I'm sorry. I'll . . ."

And then the Voice again, warmly,
"Congratulations! You get the part."

"I do? I get the part? Which one?"

"All of them. This is a one-person play, you know."

"Oh, I didn't know." Cautiously, I took a step forward. "You . . . you think I can do it?"

The Voice spoke with conviction: "For this moment you were born!"

*Barely able to breathe, I ventured,
"You'll help me?"*

"That's my job. My only job."

"You'll be my director and prompter?"

"Every step of the way!"

Butterflies again. Shyly, I grinned, suddenly it felt right, as if I had at last found my calling. "I'd like it to be really good," I said. "How long do I have to work on it?"

"Forever," said the Voice. "But I wouldn't waste any time if I were you. The world is waiting."

"Can we start now?" I asked.

"Now would be perfect," I could hear the smile. "Shall we begin?"

I took my hand down from my eyes. Perhaps I'd been growing accustomed to the light. And I thought I felt the warmth of an arm across my shoulder.

"All right," I said, "let's begin."

The curtain rises. . . .